GODZILLA

by Ian Thorne

Reprinted 1978

Library of Congress Catalog Card Number: 76-051148.

International Standard Book Numbers:
0-913940-68-2 Library Bound
0-913940-75-5 Paperback

Design - Doris Woods and Randal M. Heise.

PHOTOGRAPHIC CREDITS

Toho Studios: 2, 17, 22, 30-31, 33, 38-39, 40, 41, 42-43
Toho Studios, courtesy Forrest J. Ackerman: Cover, 6, 9, 10, 11, 12, 13, 15, 16, 24, 25, 34, 37, 47
Toho Studios, courtesy Vincent Miranda, Jr.: 18, 19, 20, 21, 26, 27, 28-29, 32, 36, 46
Toho Studios, courtesy Julian May: 44

The author gratefully acknowledges the help of Carl Jones in preparing this book.

GODZILLA

MONSTER OF THE RISING SUN

He's green! He's scaly! He's as tall as a skyscraper!

He breathes fire! He chews up trains! He stomps whole cities into rubble when he's in a bad mood!

Somehow, in spite of all this, he's very, very lovable. People all over the world have cheered him in movies and on TV. He's Godzilla, King of the Monsters.

Godzilla was created by Japanese film-makers in 1954. He was a great hit. And so he has returned again and again in a whole series of monster movies.

Godzilla has fought with many other monsters. There was Rodan, a winged reptile. There was Mothra, loveliest trouble maker in the world. These two became Godzilla's friends and helped him fight Ghidrah, a three-headed dragon.

Many other monsters inhabit the Godzilla movies. There is Godzilla's cute little son, Minya. There are lesser beasts such as spiky Anzilla, Aspiga and Gamakera the spiders, Manda the serpent, Baragon, Gorosaurus, and many more.

Godzilla has fought the giant ape, King Kong. He has battled Gigan from outer space and Hedorah the smog monster. He has even stood up to a robot version of himself!

In the beginning, Godzilla was not lovable. He was a symbol of atomic war and its horrors.

In the early 1950's, many nations were testing atomic weapons. Some people were afraid that a new war would break out. The people of Japan knew more about the effect of atomic war than any nation on earth. World War II had ended when the United States dropped atomic bombs on two Japanese cities.

A Japanese film company, Toho, made a movie about an atomic monster. The movie was a protest against atomic warfare. Its title in Japanese was Gojira. When the movie was remade for the English-speaking world, it was called Godzilla . . .

An American newspaperman, Steve Martin, lay hurt in the ruins of Tokyo. The great city, with its six million people, was nearly destroyed.

It had begun with a disaster at sea. A Japanese ship had been sunk by a strange fireball. Then more ships were destroyed.

Japanese officials hurried to Oto Island. Its people had seen fiery flashes. They claimed a long-sleeping monster had risen from the sea. The monster's name was Godzilla!

At first, scientists would not believe Godzilla existed. But then the monster appeared on the island. Testing with H-bombs had awakened it from a sleep millions of years long.

Godzilla toys with attacking airplanes.

Godzilla was 400 feet tall. The monster had radioactive breath it could spout like a flame-thrower. Ships tried to destroy Godzilla with depth bombs, but it was unharmed. It followed ships back to Tokyo Harbor and there it came ashore.

Godzilla stalked Japan's largest city. It crushed buildings like paper boxes and tried to eat a train.

Tanks and guns tried in vain to destroy Godzilla. Not even 300,000 volts of electricity could stop the atomic beast. Tokyo seemed doomed, and after that the world!

The radioactive flame-thrower breath of Godzilla burns the countryside around Tokyo.

There was only one man who had a hope of stopping Godzilla. That man was Dr. Serizawa. He had invented a dreadful new weapon, a device which removed oxygen from sea water. Any living thing within reach of the weapon would be turned to bones.

However, Serizawa had told no one of his invention except his fiancee, Imiko. The scientist was afraid evil powers would gain control of the oxygen-destroyer. It would be more dangerous to the world than the H-bomb!

Godzilla shoots fire as the field workers flee for their lives.

The gigantic Godzilla walks through buildings as if they were paper.

Imiko begged Serizawa to use the oxygen-destroyer on Godzilla. Maybe it would destroy the monster. Nothing else worked so it was worth a try.

Finally, the scientist said he would. But first, he destroyed all blueprints of his weapon. "It will be used only once," Serizawa said, "on Godzilla."

A ship took Dr. Serizawa, Imiko, and reporter Steve Martin to the part of the sea where Godzilla was hidden. Putting on a diving suit, Serizawa took his weapon into the monster's den.

Soon everything was ready. But the scientist refused to return to the surface! Instead, he watched as Godzilla approached the oxygen-destroyer. The beast set off the weapon with its mighty foot.

Those in the boat above tried to haul Serizawa up, but he had chosen to die. He was afraid evil persons would force him to reveal the secret of the oxygen-destroyer.

A geyser of water exploded upward beside the ship. Then Godzilla appeared. A monstrous scream rang out, then the scaly horror sank beneath the waves. When Godzilla reached the bottom, only a pile of bones remained.

Steve Martin radioed the news to the world: "The menace is gone, and so is a great man. But now the world can wake up and live again. Perhaps now, with the example set by Dr. Serizawa, we can do so more wisely."

Gigantis does battle with the fire breathing Armadillo.

And so the great Godzilla died. However, movie monsters that make a lot of money never die . . . and Godzilla was a blockbuster. So the monster returned.

Its head was changed slightly. It did not look so mindless, so primitive, as it had before. The second Japanese monster movie was called Gigantis, the Fire Monster.

Gigantis, a female monster, was discovered on an island. She was fighting another fire-breathing creature that resembled a spiky armadillo.

Gigantis and her apponent Anzilla, sometimes called Angorus, took their fight to Japan. The long-suffering city of Tokyo was again smashed to ruins. After a lot of huffing and puffing, Gigantis killed her rival.

At the movie's end, Gigantis retreated to a snowy island. Airplanes, bombing the slopes, started an avalanche. The she-monster was buried in the fall of ice and snow, once more destroyed "forever."

The monster-makers at Toho Studios now began to experiment with new creatures. The first was Rodan (1956).

This story began with troubles in the world's deepest mine. Workers disappeared. Later, they were found torn to pieces. The beasts responsible for the dreadful deeds finally appeared. They were giant insects left over from a prehistoric age.

A heroic miner named Shigeru finally stopped the insects by caving in the mine. Even so, worse things were lurking in the depths of the earth. An egg was getting ready to hatch!

Rodan emerges from his pre-historic egg.

The Rodan was capable of supersonic flight causing loud sonic booms.

Rodan, freshly hatched, stands ready to fly.

The miner, Shigeru, had been trapped in the cave-in. He was not hurt, and he watched a monster egg hatch. What came out was a winged reptile, something like a pteranodon. It was so big it gobbled up the giant insects as a snack!

Shigeru fled into caverns around the mine. In time, he would find his way back to the surface. Meanwhile, the winged horror made its way out of the mine. It began to fly, and to destroy.

A scientist declared that the creature was a rodan. It had lived millions of year ago. Its egg had remained safely sealed in the earth, until atomic blasts cracked the crust and admitted air and water. This allowed both the rodan and the giant insects to hatch.

The Japanese Air Force tried to destroy the winged reptile. Instead it flew from its island home, heading for the cities.

What was worse, it took its mate with it!

The two rodans attacked the city of Sasebo. They were capable of supersonic flight and the sonic booms of their passing caused buildings to topple. Fires broke out and people fled.

Fighter planes tried to shoot down the rodans. It was like mosquitoes attacking an eagle, and the two rodans did as they pleased. Finally, they flew away.

Rodan brings destruction to the city.

The Japanese scientists said the rodans were getting ready to hibernate. It was mankind's great chance! While the beasts were quiet, it might be possible to destroy them.

The two rodans were hiding in a cave on the slope of a volcano. Tanks and missiles poured explosives against the volcano. Landslides fell down the mountainside. The two flying monsters were not to be touched by their human foes.

The bombardment had another effect. It cracked the wall of the volcano. Molten lava began to gush out of the chasm. It started to engulf the cave of the rodans.

One flying reptile took wing, but the other was not quick enough. Calling to its mate, the second rodan was overcome by fumes. It fell into the lava.

The first beast refused to desert its dying mate. It returned, and both of the rodans died together in the bubbling liquid rock.

Godzilla had his hands full with many "Toho" monsters.

Rodan, like the two Godzilla movies, was a great success. The movies were enjoyed because of their special effects. The monsters did not jerk as they moved. You could not see any wires moving them, either. The craftsmen at Toho Studios made Godzilla, Gigantis, and the rodans seem alive.

Toho made another monster movie, Varan the Unbelievable, in 1958. This monster rises out of a saltwater lake and does naughty deeds until it is driven into the sea.

25

A new type of monster came from Toho in 1961. This was Mothra, a creature as charming as it was destructive.

A scientific expedition traveled from Japan to a distant island. H-bomb tests had taken place there many years before. The radioactivity had caused strange changes in the living things on the island.

The human beings were only 6 inches tall!

Greedy persons on the expedition kidnapped two tiny women. They were taken away to be displayed as freaks. The little women prayed to their guardian monster to save them.

Kidnapped native girls only 6 inches tall.

Mothra, still in caterpiller stage, destroys the Tokyo Tower. Later she makes her cocoon around it.

Mothra searches Tokyo for the 6 inch girls, destroying all in her path.

"Mothra! Mothra!" they cried.

Far away on the island, something heard! The sacred egg, which the women had guarded, hatched. Out came a huge larva. It dived into the sea and swam toward Japan.

The giant caterpillar arrived in Tokyo. It searched for its two stolen handmaids — who still sent out their mental cries. It destroyed parts of the city as it looked for the little women. Finally it came to the tall Tokyo Tower — and began to climb it!

The tower broke under the larva's weight but that did not matter. The caterpillar began to spin a huge cocoon. It rested inside, and Tokyo waited to see what would emerge.

Days later, the cocoon broke open. Out came a giant moth, its 400-foot wings softly colored. It was the biggest and the most beautiful monster of them all. No weapon could destroy it. Its wings created terrible windstorms as it searched for its handmaids.

"Mothra! Mothra!" they cried.

Finally, the creature rescued the 6-inch girls. To the relief of everyone in Tokyo, Mothra and her tiny friends returned to their faraway island.

THE RETURN OF GODZILLA

The original Godzilla was filmed in black-and-white. It was a serious horror movie. Now, Toho decided to bring back the King of the Monsters in living color. In addition, it decided to give Godzilla a sense of humor!

This would signal the beginning of a new life for the famous monster. As he became funny, he became lovable, and he became more interesting to children.

Godzilla made his comeback in the 1962 epic, King Kong Versus Godzilla. The giant ape had grown quite a bit since 1933, when he perched on a New York

King Kong and Godzilla meet for the first time.

skyscraper and swatted biplanes. By this time he was nearly the size of Godzilla.

This did not keep him from being captured. Kong was taken by raft from his secret island, to be put in a show in Japan.

Meanwhile, Godzilla's frozen sleep was broken by an atomic submarine. The beast took care of this pest, then headed for its old stomping grounds. Poor Tokyo! The two beasts met there and began to fight it out.

Who won? That depended upon where in the world you saw the movie! In the United States, King Kong came out the victor. Back in Japan, however, the home-grown monster came out on top.

Godzilla!

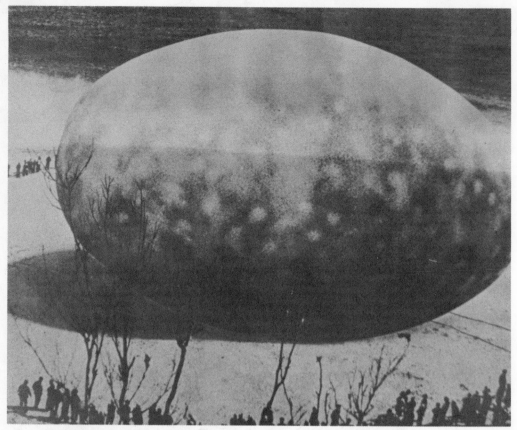

The giant "Thing" egg lays ready to hatch on the Japanese shore.

Godzilla's return was a great success. So Toho had the fire-breathing dinosaur "meet" all kinds of other super-beasts.

The next adventure was Godzilla Versus the Thing (1964). A giant egg is washed onto the Japanese shore after a hurricane. It is called the Thing. Godzilla, too, has been thrown about by the storm. He wants the egg for breakfast.

But Mama Mothra arrives to defend her child. The egg hatches. The silk of the larva traps the dinosaur and Godzilla is dumped into the sea.

Mama Mothra defends her egg from Godzilla.

Ghidrah, the three headed monster from outer space, was the most powerful foe for Godzilla and his friends.

Until now, Godzilla was definitely a bad guy. However in the next movie, Ghidrah, the Big Green monster joined the forces of law and order.

A meteor fell to earth. As it cooled, it cracked open. Out came a new and hideous monster! It was Ghidrah, a creature from outer space. It had three dragon heads. Its lightning-breath fried all enemies within spitting distance. Its batlike wings spanned hundreds of feet. It could not be hurt by even the most powerful weapons the humans could find.

What could save Earth from such a menace? None but the terrible trio — Godzilla, Rodan, and Mothra!

The giant moths tiny handmaidens were glad to call their sacred beast. But getting Rodan and Godzilla to join the fight took more convincing. Good-hearted Mothra did her best to convince them. At last, the pair agreed to join Mothra in fighting Ghidrah.

The mightiest battle yet seen in Toho-land took place on Japan's famous Mount Fuji. After a savage struggle, Mothra managed to lasso the space beast with a silken web. Then Godzilla and Rodan grabbed Ghidrah and dumped it over a cliff.

Deeply ashamed, Ghidrah retreated into the blackness of space. Until the next time!

Ghidrah wasted no time in getting its revenge. Monster Zero (1965) told of a new planet entering the Solar System. The sneaky folk of this world asked to "borrow" Godzilla and Rodan to fight Ghidrah. (The three-headed dragon was now holed up on Planet X.)

Kindly earthlings let the friendly beasts go, only to discover it was all a trick! Planet X hoped to enslave Earth with the help of Ghidrah. Of course, our planet's monsters don't take this calmly. It was monster against monster, together with a great deal of space warfare.

When the smoke cleared away, guess who won?

Earth monsters are sent to Planet X.

Godzilla and Rodan battle the fierce Ghidrah on Planet X.

By this time, the Toho monster movies had a light-hearted flavor. They were being played more and more for laughs. The monsters themselves were in on the joke, and lovable Godzilla was the most funny of all.

In 1966, he was the winner over a lobster-like monster in Godzilla Versus the Sea Monster.

Shortly after, Son of Godzilla reached movie

houses. The monster's child was a fat little fellow who looked like a cross between a dinosaur and the Pillsbury dough-boy. Little Minya was unable to breathe fire like his dad. He could only puff smoke rings! Nevertheless, both father and son fought and won over giant mantises, the latest in the endless list of Toho monsters.

By the late 1960's, there were so many Japanese monsters at large, it was hard to keep track of them all. It was time for a new film:

Destroy All Monsters.

The story is laid in the year 2000. By then, all monsters had been rounded up and sent to the island of Ogsawara. Electronic barriers kept the beasts from escaping.

But Kilaaks from outer space free the monsters and send them to destroy Earth's cities. Godzilla crushes New York. Mothra smashes Peking. Rodan topples Moscow, and so it goes.

"All the great monsters together for one movie."

Meanwhile, the alien Kilaaks are doing their secret work. The monster attacks are merely a trick. The Kilaaks are working to make slaves of Earth's people.

Clever scientists manage to turn the monsters against the invading Kilaaks. In a last-ditch effort, the aliens bring in Ghidrah to fight on their side. It is good monsters against bad. Once again cities fall, the Earth quakes, and a wonderful time is had by young movie-goers all over the world.

Our planet is saved, at least for awhile.

Godzilla fights off the Smog Monster.

Not all of the Godzilla movies were slam-bang action films. One of them, Godzilla's Revenge, was a strange and touching story.

A sad little boy named Kenji is neglected by his parents. He daydreams a visit to Monster Island. There Godzilla's son, Minya, befriends him. The boy has a wonderful time visiting with all the monsters . . .

Then he wakes up. Back in the real world, Kenji is kidnapped by robbers. But Minya has taught him that even small people can be brave. So Kenji escapes, the robbers are caught, and the boy's parents resolve never to neglect him again.

Godzilla would meet many more monsters. The children of the world never seem to get tired of his adventures.

In Godzilla Versus Gigan, he battled against another beast from outer space. This one was controlled by intelligent cockroaches.

In Godzilla Versus Megalon, his foes were monsters from the evil kingdom of Seatopia. The Big Green won out with the help of a robot friend.

Then came Godzilla Versus the Smog Monster. Dreadful Hedorah, a walking blob, was spawned from pollution. Godzilla struck Japan's blow for ecology.

The next picture, released in 1976, pitted the Scaly Champ against a robot version of himself. It was entitled Godzilla Versus Mechagodzilla.

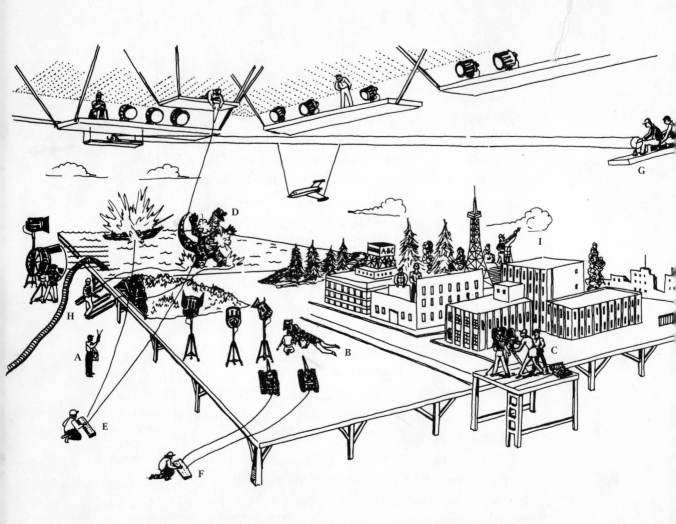

This diagram shows steps in the making of a Godzilla movie. The director (A) coordinates action with a walkie-talkie. Close-up cameramen (B) and long-shot cameramen (C) film the action as an actor in a Godzilla suit (D) performs. Special effects man (E) sets off tiny explosions. Another man (F) operates model tanks. Airplane is operated by wires (G). Wind and wave machines (H) take care of water effects. Technicians (I) ready a miniature city set for Godzilla to destroy.

44

The man who created Godzilla, and most of the other wonderful monsters as well, was named Eiji Tsuburaya. He began making films when he was just a little boy. Later he became a cameraman, then a special-effects wizard for Toho Studios.

There are several different ways of making movie monsters. King Kong and many other American made monsters use "stop-motion" photography. In it, a small model monster is moved little by little, and the movie shot one frame at a time. When the film is speeded up, the monster moves. However, even in the most skillful stop-motion, the movement is jerky. Tsuburaya wanted his monsters to move smoothly.

He used two different kinds of monsters to bring Godzilla to life. In some scenes, Godzilla is a small model, operated by electrical motors. In others, he is an actor dressed in a carefully made monster costume.

Godzilla looks real because the actor stands among beautifully made miniature buildings, trees, cars, and trains. The cameraman shoots the scene from a low angle. He aims his lens up at Godzilla. In the finished film, viewers have the effect of a beast hundreds of feet tall destroying a real city.

Eiji Tsuburaya died in 1969, during the making of Godzilla's Revenge. But other people carry on his work and the movie monsters he created may never die.

Some people have said that the Godzilla movies are like a comic book, and so they are, but what's wrong with that? Many other critics have enjoyed the movies. Their special effects are wonderful. And the plots are almost always good fun for both adults and children.

It doesn't matter that all Godzilla's actions aren't realistic. Millions of people, all around the world, wouldn't miss a monstrous moment of them.

One movie featured a machanical Godzilla.

Godzilla's creator, the late Eiji Tsuburaya, checks over the actor wearing the Godzilla suit.